"I can't talk,
I've got
FARBLES
in my mouth!"

For Frank and Carrie

I can't talk, I've got Farbles in my mouth
Text copyright © 1995 by Mary Vigliante Szydlowski.
Illustrations copyright © 1995 by Ray Dirgo.
Typography by Alicia Mikles.
Published by Greene Bark Press Inc.,
PO Box 1108 Bridgeport, CT 06601-1108

Library of Congress Catalog # 95-078161
Library of Congress Cataloging in Publication Data
    Szydlowski, Mary Vigliante
    I can't talk, I've got Farbles in my mouth
    Summary: Boy awakens to find a family of
Farbles has taken up temporary residence in his mouth.
His quest is to find them a more permanent home.
    1. Children's Stories, American. [1. Mouth-Fiction]
    1. Dirgo, Ray, ill 11. Title
    ISBN 1-880851-21-0

"I can't talk, I've got FARBLES in my mouth!"

WRITTEN BY **Mary Vigliante Szydlowski**

ILLUSTRATED BY **Ray Dirgo**

GREENE BARK PRESS, INC.
P.O. Box 1108
Bridgeport, CT 06601-1108

James Edward Beechum was very neat. He made his bed every morning, hung up his clothes and kept his room clean. He took a bath every night and washed his hands and face before meals.

But most of all, he took care of his teeth. He brushed them first thing in the morning, after every meal and snack, and before he went to bed at night. He flossed and rinsed too. James visited his dentist every six months for a check—up. He'd never had a cavity. James wanted to be a dentist when he grew up. He knew the names of all the teeth in his mouth: the incisors, canines, bicuspids and molars; and he knew which ones were which.

James Edward Beechum was very neat...

The problems with his mouth began when they started repairing the bandstand in the park across from his house. The workers were replacing the old roof, fixing the floor, stairs and the railings, and giving everything a new coat of paint. James had watched the workman dig up the white pebble path around the bandstand and pile the tiny stones under a tree.

James felt a tickle on his tongue, like something was crawling on it. He jumped out of bed and ran to the mirror to see what it was.

He opened his mouth and looked inside. "Eeek!" he screamed. Fuzzy green things were stuck between his teeth and on his tongue. They looked like bits of spinach. He brushed his teeth, flossed, rinsed and brushed some more, but couldn't get rid of them. When he brushed the left side, the green stuff moved to the right. When he did the right, they went left.

"What is going on in there?" he yelled.

He was shocked when a voice squeeked "Hello!"

James looked around to see who'd said it, but he was alone. Where was the voice coming from? "Is there someone here?" he asked nervously.

"It's just us," a chorus of voices responded.

"Us?" repeated James, looking bewildered. The voices were coming from inside his mouth.

James ran to get a magnifying glass. When he got back, he opened his mouth and peered inside. He couldn't believe his eyes. Little green creatures with pointy ears and big eyes were waving at him. They looked like carpet fuzz with chubby arms and legs, pug noses, and stubby tails.

"Who are you?" James demanded, "And what are you doing in my mouth?"

"We're Farbles," the fattest one said. "I'm Burt, and this is my wife Gert and the girls: Sal, Tish, Jane, Barb, May, Dee, Fay and Lee, and the boys: Roy, Ray, Jay, Ed, Fred, Sam, Jed and Ben. And over there is Grandpa Stan and Grannie Em and Gert's folks Grandpa Zac and Grandma Sue and Uncle Zeke and Auntie Lou and of course the baby, little Irwin."

"Excuse me," said James sternly, "But just what do you think you're doing in my mouth?"

"We're living here," said Burt.

"YOU'RE WHAT?"

"It's only temporary," said Gert, "Just until they put our house back."

"What house?"

"We lived in the pebble path in the park. One morning some rude men dug up our home," complained Gert. "We had all we could do to save our belongings before being dumped on the street."

"Then we saw you," said Burt, "Your teeth looked like pebbles."

"But you can't stay here," James protested, "This is my mouth, not a house. I use it myself. I talk with it, eat with it, drink with it. Move someplace else!"

"Can't," said Burt.

"Why not?"

"We've no place else'to go!"

"Well you can't stay here," James informed him.

A minute passed, then two, but they didn't leave.

"I'm going to tell my mother," James threatened, "She'll throw you out!" When they still didn't go, he hurried off to find her.

His mother was working at her desk.

"Muffer, umfing awful ith dowing on," James looked horrified; he couldn't talk right. The Farbles were tickling his tonsils and jumping on his tongue.

"What did you say dear?" his mother asked. "I couldn't understand you."

James pointed to his mouth, "Farbles," he said.

"James stop mumbling."

"I can't tawt. I dot Farbles in my mout."

"Marbles in your mouth?" His mother repeated, wondering if she'd heard him right, "Spit them out this instant; you could choke."

"Aargh," James muttered in frustration. He grabbed a pencil, scrawling a note across a paper she was writing on. "A FAMILY OF FARBLES MOVED INTO MY MOUTH," it said.

His mother frowned. "I've no time for jokes," she scolded, "I'm busy." Mother was an accountant. She didn't like being interrupted when she was working. "Out!" she said, pointing to the door.

James spent the rest of the day trying to evict the Farbles. He ate six times, hoping that having egg salad and hot chili, lumpy oatmeal and tomato soup dumped on them would make them want to leave, but it didn't. He drank gallons of soda, hoping the bubbles would drive them away, but they stayed put. It was nearly bedtime when he came up with a sure-fire way to send them packing . . . the waterpik.

"I'll get you now," he announced, aiming the nozzle at his teeth that he had brushed for the tenth time.

He shot a jet of water into his mouth, but instead of running away, they just stood there. A few seconds later they were covered with foam. They were showering!

James gave up! How was he ever going to get rid of them?

James woke up in the middle of the night; something was pinching his tongue.

"Close your mouth," Burt Farble yelled, "You're letting in a draft."

James didn't get a wink of sleep the rest of the night.

He could hardly stay awake the next day. He walked around with his eyes half closed, trying to figure out a way to rid himself of those pesky Farbles, but he was so tired he couldn't think straight.

That night he went to bed early, but couldn't sleep. His head was pounding. He thought he had a headache, but then realized he was hearing drums. "The music is too loud! Turn it down!" he demanded.

James went to the park the following morning. He looked awful. He had dark circles under his eyes. He hadn't slept again.

He was looking for a place to leave the Farbles.

James took a bucket of pebbles from the pile and dumped them by a tree, then spread them out on the grass.

"What are you doing?" asked Tish Farble, who, with her sisters and brothers was sunning herself on James' nose and chin. They looked like green pimples.

"I'm making you a house," said James.

Burt watched from James' bottom lip. "Our path had several layers of pebbles to protect us when people walked or rode their bikes over us," he said.

"This is good enough," yelled James.

"There aren't enough layers," protested Gert, who'd joined her husband.

"I don't care!" screamed James, "I just want you out."

"Well we know where we're not wanted," sniffed Gert. "We'll be gone within the hour."

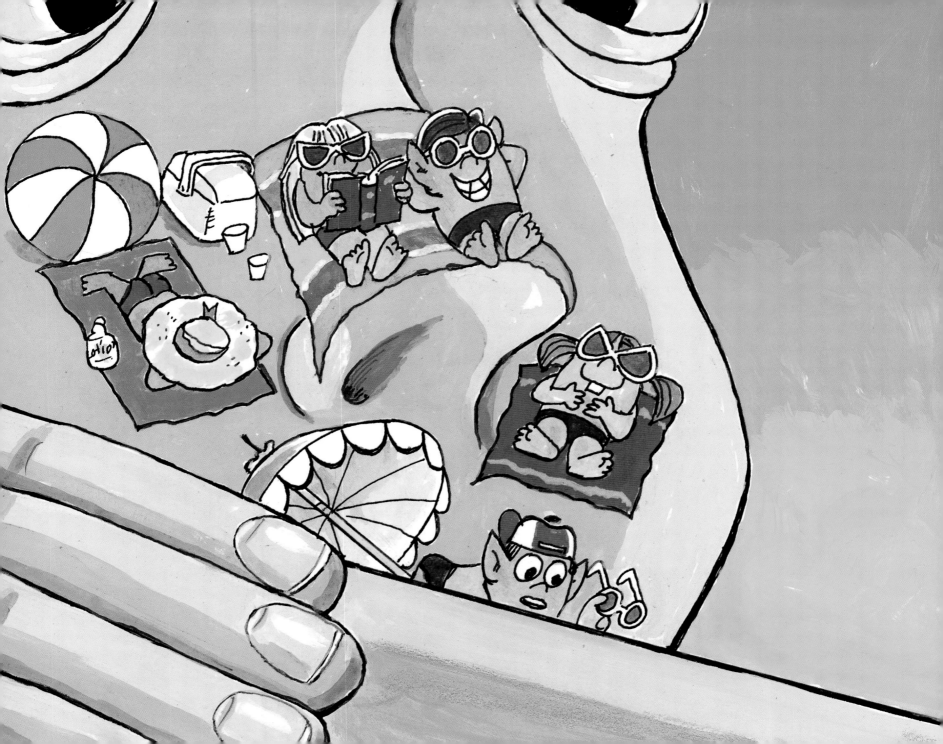

James jumped for joy when the Farbles left, but his happiness didn't last long.

He was about to leave the park when a fat lady and her chubby husband decided to sit under the tree.

"STOP! You'll squish them!" James screamed

"Squish what?" the woman asked.

"Bees," James lied .

The lady looked scared.

"A whole hive of them."

The couple hurried away.

James decided it was too dangerous to leave the Farbles there. They might get run over, stomped or sat on. He'd have to put up with them a while longer, until he could find them a better home.

That night he felt something kick his tonsils.

"What are you doing?" he whispered, half asleep.

"Trying to get you to stop snoring," someone shouted. "You're keeping us awake with all your snorting."

"Sorry," James apologized .

Though he tried, he couldn't get back to sleep.

By morning he was exhausted and had bags under his eyes.

That day, James tried to find another home for the Farbles.

He put them on the pebble banks of a brook, but had to rescue them three hours later when a heavy rain storm almost washed them away. He got soaked, caught a cold and stayed up all night sneezing.

He took them to a rock quarry, thinking they'd like it there, but they hated it. They complained about the dust and noise from the steamshovels and bulldozers.

James bought a bag of stone chips from the lawn and garden store and put it in the shed. They didn't like that either.

"Too dark," they complained.

So he moved it into the sunshine. Then they complained that the neighbor's dog was sniffing and pawing the bag. There was no pleasing them!

One night the Farbles woke him at 4 a.m., demanding he gargle with strong mouthwash.

"No more garlic dip for you young man," Gert said, "Your breath is awful!"

James was getting so little sleep that he was dead-tired all the time. He fell asleep at breakfast one day, napped at lunch the next and slept through dinner the day after that. He even fell asleep during baseball practice.

His parents were worried about him. Not only was he not sleeping well, but he was continually mumbling to himself.

One afternoon James fell asleep on the backyard swing. The next thing he knew smoke was rising from his nose. He crossed his eyes to see what it was. There was a barbecue grill there and a hundred Farbles he'd never seen before walking around on his face.

James ranted and raved, demanding they leave, but no one listened. He got so mad he ran to a closet to sulk, but came out after the Farbles threatened to build a bonfire on his upper lip.

He pouted while they partied.

He couldn't imagine things getting worse, but they did!

James awoke at half-past six one morning to find green Farbles all over his body.

"What now?" he asked, trying to brush them away with his hand.

"It's awful," Burt wailed, "They're replacing all our lovely pebble paths with cement sidewalks. Now all the Farbles are homeless! Can everyone stay here until we find a new place to live?"

The last thing James needed was more Farbles! But he felt sorry for them and agreed to let them move in too.

Living conditions were cramped. James looked like a chipmunk, his cheeks bulging, but what could he do, the Farbles had no place else to go.

He'd just nodded off to sleep when a baby Farble woke him up with his crying. He lay awake, unable to sleep when suddenly it came to him . . . a plan to get the Farbles back their homes.

He would write a petition asking the city to keep the pebble path in the park.

He began working on it the next morning. Everybody signed: relatives, neighbors, people on the street corners, even shoppers coming out of the department and grocery stores downtown.

After receiving the petition, the city managers decided the pebble paths could stay.

The bandstand was finished in time for the first summer concert.
The pebble paths had been reset and raked that afternoon.

The time had come, the Farbles were leaving, going home.
They'd been so busy moving their things, they hadn't even had time
to say "Thank you" to James. They'd just waved good by as they
disappeared under the pebbles.

James got ready to go to the concert. He went to the mirror to brush his teeth and was surprised at what he saw in his reflection. His teeth looked beautiful. They were sparkling white. The Farbles had brushed, cleaned, flossed, and polished them until they gleamed. They had also scrawled a note on his tongue. "THANK YOU!" it said, "Love, your friends, the Farbles."